Sallie Stephenson

CRESTWOOD HOUSE
New York

Maxwell Macmillan Canada
Toronto

Maxwell Macmillan International
New York   Oxford   Singapore   Sydney

Photo Credits
Cover: Daytona International Speedway
Brian McLeod: 4, 7, 18, 19, 23, 24, 25, 28, 31, 32, 33, 37, 38, 41
Curtis "Crawfish" Crider: 9, 12, 34
Sallie Stephenson: 11
Howe Racing Enterprises: 20
Wendy Southard: 27
Jim Jones/Halifax photos: 40

Acknowledgments
I would like to give special thanks to race car drivers Alice ("Racing Granny") Tatroe, Duke Southard, Curtis Crawford, Connie Saylor and Patty Moise for helping in the research of this book.

Copyright © 1991 by Crestwood House, Macmillan Publishing Company

Crestwood House
Macmillan Publishing Company
866 Third Avenue
New York, NY 10022

Maxwell Macmillan Canada, Inc.
1200 Eglinton Avenue East
Suite 200
Don Mills, Ontario M3C 3N1

Macmillan Publishing Company is part of the Maxwell Communication Group of Companies.

First edition

Printed in the United States of America

10   9   8   7   6   5   4   3   2   1

Stephenson, Sallie.
    Circle track racing/by Sallie Stephenson.—1st ed.
        p.   cm.—(Fast track)
    Includes bibliographical references (p.) and index.
    Summary: Includes all aspects of circle track racing: history, skills needed, driver responsibilities, safety equipment, etc.
        ISBN 0-89686-693-9
        1. Stock car racing—United States—History—Juvenile literature.
[1. Stock car racing.] I. Title. II. Series: Stephenson, Sallie.
Fast track.
GV1029.9.S74S74   1991
796.7'2'0973—dc20
                                                                    91-11541

INTRODUCTION

SPOTLIGHT ON THE DRIVER

BEHIND THE SCENES

The First Time

The first time on the race track isn't easy. Your foot shakes on the gas pedal as you rev up the engine. You ask yourself, "What am I doing here?" Even the short track, not nearly as large as a superspeedway, looks big the first time you see it from behind the wheel of a car. The rest of the cars look huge too.

The other racers finish their practice laps. Now you all line up to begin the important **qualifying rounds,** or timed laps. How well you do in the timed laps determines whether you can enter the main event, or feature race. It also determines your starting position.

As you drive around the track you don't think about the fans. You concentrate on keeping out of trouble and finishing with a good time. You

◀ A driver waits for his race to start.

feel as if you're going fast, but other cars are whizzing by on both sides.

You get through the timed laps and manage to qualify for the feature race. You're placed in the third from last position.

After going over your car one last time with your **pit crew**, you drive into position. While waiting for the race to start, you think about all the hard work it took to get here. The hours practicing on the track and working in the garage were long. But now you're ready for your first big race.

The **pace car** heads out and you follow it along with the other cars. The pace car circles the track several times. Each time you near the flagman you watch to see if he is going to wave and drop the green flag, which means the race has begun. On your next turn around you see the flag fall. Immediately you hit the gas pedal. There is a deafening roar as the other drivers **accelerate**. The race is on!

As you circle the track you look for openings in the pack of cars swarming around you. Some cars pull ahead. If you are quick enough, you can squeeze into the spaces they leave. Slowly you move past the other racers.

After 20 laps, you pull into the pit area. Your pit crew rushes over to check your tires and make small adjustments to your engine. Someone hands you a drink of water through

A member of a pit crew secures a tire before a race.

the window. It is extremely hot in the car. You spend only moments in the pit.

Then you pull out onto the track again and rejoin the race. On lap 49 you see the flagman wave the white flag. You have one more lap to go. You step on the gas and pull ahead of another car. On the last turn, you can see the finish line and the flagman waiting with the checkered flag. There are several cars still ahead of you. You look for an opening.

But the cars in front of you stay tightly together. You finish the race in sixth place.

As you get out of the car, your crew runs over to congratulate you. You didn't win. But you did very well for your first race. You're already thinking about the next one.

The Start of It All

Back in the 1920s it was against the law to buy or sell alcohol. It was the time of Prohibition. There were no bars or liquor stores.

Bootleggers made illegal liquor called moonshine. They were called bootleggers because they would hide the bottles of moonshine in their high boots if a policeman was around. They drove fast cars to deliver it to customers.

These bootleggers were always on the lookout for the police. If they were caught, they would go to jail. To avoid the police, they would deliver their alcohol at night. Back then, roads were narrower and more twisty and crooked than they are today. If a bootlegger met a police car at night, he would turn his car around quickly and race in the other direction. This fast getaway spin became known as the "bootleg turn."

Prohibition laws were abolished nationwide in 1933. But some southern states still had laws against making or buying liquor. In the 1930s and 1940s bootleggers made a lot of money by making only five or six deliveries a week.

Bootleggers in the South were proud of how fast their cars ran. They had powerful engines specially built. They used hot-rod parts so that their old **jalopies** could outrun police cars.

Sometimes bootleggers held races in cow pastures to see whose car ran the fastest. As many as 30 or 40 bootleggers would show up. They would drive their cars around and around the pasture to make a circular track about half a mile around. They made bets against each other. Then they raced their cars around the circle to see who could drive the fastest.

People would see the clouds of dust caused by these races. Many came to watch what was going on. The drivers wore old football helmets for protection during races. One racer would pass a helmet around. The people watching would throw in nickels and dimes. This money

In the early days of circle track racing, accidents were very common. Here a car has gone through a fence surrounding a field.

was added to the bet money and given to the winner of the race. This money was called the **purse**.

Many bootleggers raced for money in cow pastures during the day and ran whiskey at night. They were daredevils. They drove quickly and recklessly. They raced ordinary cars on ordinary Sears Roebuck tires. But their cars were customized to run fast. Some went as fast as 80 miles per hour on those first dirt tracks.

These illegal races soon became public events. Grandstands were built for the fans. Tickets were sold and prize money was awarded to the winner. The old souped-up jalopies used by the bootleggers were replaced by **modifieds,** cars that were specially designed for racing. Then the dirt tracks were replaced by asphalt tracks. And the old bootlegging drivers were replaced by professional racers. Circle track racing was born.

The Early Days

Today circle track races are held on asphalt tracks. But the story of this type of car racing begins on dirt.

Dirt track racing was especially popular in the south after World War II. Many small towns and villages were connected by networks of narrow,

Many early circle track races were held on simple dirt tracks.

twisting roads. Cars were the only form of transportation available to most people. People liked to see how fast their cars could go on these roads. Dirt track races offered the same kind of excitement to rural audiences. Racing soon became very popular.

Some early dirt tracks, like Pennsboro Motor Speedway near Parkersburg, West Virginia, were converted horse tracks. Racing fans brought shovels to carve out a grandstand from the side of the mountain overlooking the track. This track is still in operation but now runs only what racers call "high-dollar" events.

A race held on August 23, 1947, at the Greensboro, North Carolina, speedway is typical of an early race. The feature race was a 50-lap event. The grand prize was $500. A few of the rules were:

1. All cars must have a full windshield.
2. All models of cars made from 1937 to 1947 are eligible.
3. All cars must have **hydraulic brakes**.
4. Ford and Mercury **carburetors** may be interchanged.
5. Any wheel size may be used.
6. A stock, or standard, **ignition and coil** must be used.
7. Any kind of spark plug may be used.
8. Springs may be reinforced.

An early NASCAR race in Darlington, South Carolina.

The cars at these races were **stock cars**. A stock car has the same body and frame as one that comes off the assembly line. But the insides are altered to make the car run faster.

Another favorite track in the early days of stock car racing was the Cowpens Speedway off Highway 29 in Spartanburg, South Carolina. On a Friday night 75 to 80 cars would show up to race. Fords were the most popular cars. They were fast and durable. And they were equipped with new V-8 engines, with eight cylinders instead of four. The cylinders were in a V-formation, four on each side. These powerful cars dominated the speedway.

Grandstands would be packed for races. You could ask any kid if he or she wanted to be a race car driver and the answer would be a loud "Yes!" It was not unusual to see drivers as young as 15 or 16 years old. Drivers would drift into **broadslide** turns, sweeping around the dirt track, knocking fenders with other drivers and sending up clouds of dust.

Cars threw dirt everywhere. It flew into the grandstands. It got into people's eyes, up their noses and all over their clothes. Race promoters knew that true racing fans would put up with anything to watch.

But with all that dirt flying around, it was hard for the drivers to see ahead of their own cars. And many dirt races were held at night, which made driving—and watching—even more dangerous.

On June 19, 1949, the first Grand National race was held at the old Charlotte Speedway in North Carolina. This was the first race that featured late-model race cars, cars that were no more than three years old. These were unmodified passenger cars that had come right off the Detroit assembly lines. Even the tires were standard street tires.

Automobile manufacturers found that these races were great opportunities to show off their new car lines. These cars would soon become available to the public in dealers' showrooms. Fans would come to the races to see the newest models. Then they could go out and buy the same cars they'd seen racing around the track!

At first, the unmodified cars could not stand up to the demands of racing. The windshield might pop loose, an axle might break, or the engine might overheat. The late-model production-line cars were not nearly as stable as the modified hot rods and jalopies of the past.

Over time, race car engineering improved. Mechanics figured out all sorts of ways to increase performance. They learned how to cool engines and how to reinforce a car's suspension so it wouldn't bend or buckle during sharp turns. And they learned to adjust a car's weight so that the right front wheels wouldn't fly off or burst during hairpin turns.

In 1949 the National Association for Stock Car Auto Racing (NASCAR) was formed to organize these races. It set up rules and regulations. It established different racing classes. Interest grew in promoting these popular, moneymaking events. New tracks sprang up all over the country.

In the 1950s and 1960s stock car racing became increasingly popular. Weekly races were big events. Some of those early racers, such as Speedy Thompson, Fireball Roberts and Red Byron, have become legends in the racing world.

By the late 1970s, the constant upkeep of the dirt surfaces had become too expensive for track owners. By the 1980s, most of the dirt tracks were closed or were resurfaced with asphalt. Yet some dirt tracks, like the Eldora Speedway in Ohio, are still open. With its extremely high banks and sharp turns, Eldora challenges even the most skilled drivers. It is the site of the World 100, which draws over 200 dirt track drivers and 15,000 fans every year.

A lot of stock car drivers who have made it all the way to the top of the sport, the highly professional Winston Cup series, got their start on dirt tracks. There, they proved that they had the skill and determination to make it in big-time stock car racing. Baseball players must play in the bush leagues before they hit the majors. In the same way, stock car racers learn the fundamentals of their sport on dirt or sandlot tracks before racing in NASCAR events.

Racing Today

Today there are different divisions, or classes, of race cars that compete in circle track races. One track may be used for a particular type of race or kind of car. It depends on the type of track.

Whatever kind of race it is, the basic rules are the same. Every driver runs practice laps. After the practice laps, the qualifying rounds are held. There are competitions to determine which drivers will be allowed to race and which starting positions they will get. Each driver runs his or her car around the track once as fast as possible. Each lap is timed by an official. Those cars with the fastest times are allowed to race in the main, or feature, race. The number of cars that are allowed to race in the feature event varies from race to race.

After qualifying, the cars are weighed by safety inspectors. They make sure that each car

meets the legal requirements. Then the drivers line up according to their qualifying times. The car with the fastest time is in first position, the second fastest is in second position, and so on.

The pace car leads the racers around the track several times. All the cars must stay behind the pace car. Then the pace car leaves the track and the flagman waves a green flag. This signals the start of the race.

Races are made up of a number of laps, or times around the track. The winner is the person who completes the required number of laps in the fastest time. Winners receive trophies,

Previous page: A circle track race draws teams from all over the country.

The chassis of a late-model car.

money and points. These points are added up at the end of the racing season to determine who are the best drivers. Racers are then ranked according to the number of points they have earned. The driver with the most points is number one.

No matter what division a driver races in, the car he or she drives is called a stock car. This means that the car has a standard, or stock, body like any ordinary car. The difference is that the engine, wheels and body have been modified to make the car lighter and go faster. A stock car may begin as an old Trans-Am, a rebuilt Mustang or a brand-new Ford. But only the newest of these cars are called late-model cars.

Not everyone who wants to compete in circle track racing can afford a late-model car. They can cost as much as $35,000 to build. The most expensive part of a late-model race car is the engine. It represents nearly half the total price of a race car. The rest of the cost is in the **chassis**, body and specialized parts. The bodies of late-model cars driven in dirt track racing used to be made of sheet metal. Now most are made of fiberglass.

Other popular stock cars are called mini-stocks. In recent years Volvos, Volkswagen "Bugs" and Mini Coopers were used in mini-stock racing. Now Chevrolet Vegas and Ford

Pintos are raced. These compact cars were popular in the 1970s. They turn up at junkyards, and parts can still be found for them. Most builders of mini-stocks remove the rear window so that air can flow through the car. This reduces wind resistance and helps the car go faster. Adding **exhaust headers** and a carburetor with higher air and fuel intake gives the engine more **horsepower** to make it go faster.

Midgets are another type of car used in circle track racing. They look like big-engine go-carts with metal cages built around them to protect the drivers. These small cars have no ignition starters. They have to be pushed by another vehicle to get the engine going. They are a special treat for the fans.

What It Takes to Get into Circle Track Racing

Stock car racing began in the 1930s. You could get started in racing for as little as $1,000. Many drivers rescued rusting cars from junkyards and turned them into race cars. This took many hours of work. They would have to fine-tune or even rebuild engines. They would add heavy-duty shock absorbers and springs to pro-

A late-model car like this one can cost as much as $70,000.

tect their cars from the rough race courses. And they would make changes to the cars so that they could go fast on the track.

The first stock car drivers made seat belts out of rope. They kept the doors closed with a leather belt or chains. This was to prevent doors from flying open during the races. If they were good mechanics, they might specially grind the camshaft. Or they might add extra carburetors to the engine or use different gears—depending on which track they were racing.

In the 1960s you could build a race car for between $6,000 and $8,000. For that you could expect to get a winning car. Now a race car powerful enough to win at the Daytona superspeedway costs more than $70,000! Body designs are always changing. New styles are designed to produce faster cars.

A good way to get started in racing is through street stock racing. This is a class made for people just starting out so that they can decide whether they like racing. Street stocks are full-sized cars that were manufactured during the late 1960s and early 1970s. These cars usually look as if they were hauled from a junkyard. They probably were! Many times a racer will get a car from a junkyard and add only the barest essentials to get the car around a track. A racer may spend as little as $2,000 to fix up a car. But looks can be deceiving. The most battered car may seem as if it won't even make it around the track. But it may be a winner.

Everyone wants to break into late-model racing and move up the ladder by winning more races. Reaching the status of a Winston Cup

The driver of this car advertises for a sponsor by putting a sticker on his door.

Getting a sponsor helps a driver cover the costs of racing. This car is sponsored by Interstate Batteries.

driver is the dream of drivers all around the country. But this takes tens of thousands of dollars.

To get this money, drivers need **sponsors**. A sponsor is a person or company that gives racers money in exchange for publicity. For example, a soft-drink company might decide to sponsor a racer. The company will look for someone who has won frequently or who shows signs of becoming a winning driver. The company will then give the driver the money he or she needs to get a good car, hire a fine pit crew, and pay for other expenses. In return, the company's logo will be painted on the car. Maybe the driver will do promotions for the soft drink. Every time the driver races, thousands of fans will see the company's advertising on the car. They might then associate the soft drink with the racer and buy the soft drink. That way, the company makes money and the driver can afford to continue racing.

The sponsor is very important to a driver. You need money to have a car built, to repair it, to make improvements, to replace tires and worn parts, and to keep it running. The more money you receive from sponsors, the more chances you have to win.

Skills for Circle Track Racing

Money is not the only thing a racer needs. It takes great skill to drive a race car. Circle track races aren't won simply by driving fast. Strategy and quick thinking developed over years of driving are also needed. Most race car drivers eat, think and sleep racing.

It takes a lot of mental concentration and physical stamina to compete on a race track. A driver needs upper-body strength to handle the quick turns. Like all athletes, drivers must exercise to develop strength in their arms and shoulders.

Fast reflexes are also important. Everything

happens quickly in racing. You must be able to see trouble ahead and react in a split second. You must know at all times what is happening in front, behind and to the sides of your car. A driver must develop a sense of how a race runs, and what the other racers are doing. There isn't time to keep looking in the rearview mirror. It takes experience to develop this ability.

When driving a race car there are many things to remember. A good racer must develop and refine a driving technique. You must learn how to go into a turn without letting the car behind pass in front of you. You must be able to speed

A racer learns the fine points of driving at Southard's School of High-Performance Driving.

Accidents like this one can happen suddenly during a race. Drivers must always be on the lookout for trouble signs.

up coming out of a turn so you don't lose time. You have to develop a smooth rhythm when moving your foot between the gas pedal and the brake so that your car runs gracefully. And you must learn how to adjust your steering if your car goes into a spin or if a tire blows out.

To learn all these things, many racers attend driving schools. There, an instructor can also teach you how to set up your race car for better handling on the track. The instructor watches the way you drive and offers suggestions for refining your technique.

Another way to learn how to drive is by talking to other racers and watching them drive. You may also want to become part of a pit crew for an established driver. This way you learn firsthand what it takes to race successfully. You can ask questions of people who have been racing for a long time. Racers love what they do. They are generally happy to share their experiences with new drivers. But be careful—they may pass on bad habits!

A Driver's Responsibilities

A driver needs to know how his or her car handles—including the sounds the car makes at every speed. The driver must adapt to the rhythms of both the car and the races. That's why there are practice laps before a feature. This gives the racer time to look, listen and feel for anything unusual in the way the car is handling.

On local tracks, a driver may be riding solo. He or she may have to be the car's mechanic. The driver has to know the car inside and out.

The driver's knowledge and skill could mean the difference between life and death.

Sometimes a driver will ask an expert for advice. This expert may have worked on cars in the upper divisions, like the Winston Cup races. The expert will come to the track and check the way the car is set up. This expert will also watch the way the racer drives and make suggestions to improve technique.

This kind of expert is called an **efficiency expert**. He does many things. He looks the car over. He times the car with a stopwatch to see if the driver is going as fast as possible. He listens to the car's engine and checks for any problems.

When you are racing, you are responsible for your own safety as well as the safety of those racing with you. That's why it is so important to make sure your car is running well. You don't want to be the cause of an accident because of something that should have been fixed after the practice laps.

Unfortunately, not all drivers are responsible. Most are, but some simply want to get out on the track and drive. That's why tracks have safety inspectors, people who look over the cars right before a race to make sure that there are no

▶ A driver makes a last-minute adjustment on his car.

During a circle track race, cars can run very close together, so it is important for drivers to be aware of what is going on around them.

obvious safety hazards. But safety inspectors can't catch everything. That's why each racer must ensure that his or her car is as safe as possible. Circle track racing is fast and exciting. But it should also be safe. An accident ruins the fun for everyone.

Safety Equipment

You're eighth in the starting position for a 50-lap feature race. You're following the pace car. It leaves the track. You see the green flag drop. Everyone's racing.

Three-fourths of the way through the race, you've moved up to third place. Six, seven laps go by. Now you're in second. You're riding the bumper of the first-place driver. She's leading the way toward the slower cars that lag behind. Now she catches up with and passes through them. You follow her through.

You keep your position until the 47th lap. Now you see that another car is closing in behind you. You can see the driver in your rear-view mirror. But you think you can keep ahead of him and pass the first-place car during the last lap.

In the pit area race teams get their cars ready for competition.

This huge pileup at the New Smyrna Speedway in Florida happened when a car lost control and the drivers couldn't get out of the way.

All of a sudden something unplanned happens. The driver in first place blows a tire. You're following right behind her. You can't react quickly enough. You hit her bumper and spin out. The car that was behind you speeds by and wins the race.

That was a hazard you hadn't counted on. But in racing, cars fail to finish for many reasons. The driver may crash. You may blow an engine or transmission. At another time, the engine may catch on fire. Anything can happen in racing.

Over the years, people connected with racing have developed many ways to protect the drivers and cars from accidents. Crash helmets, then seat belts and **roll bars** became required. Racers started equipping their cars with heavy-duty suspension systems. They built safety shields around fuel tanks. Fire extinguishers also became standard equipment. As the cars became faster, they also became safer.

Drivers today wear fire-retardant clothing. Their suits, socks, shoes and even their underwear are designed to protect their bodies from fire. In the old days drivers wore no such protection. Now each race track has an emergency crew trained to deal with accidents and fires. Whatever happens on the track, someone is always there to handle it.

The People Who Make It Happen

The driver is the most visible person at a race. But there are many people working behind the scenes who are just as important. Everyone involved in building a race car works together.

The owner or sponsor provides the racing team with money. He or she makes it possible for the car to be built and the racer to compete.

The people responsible for making sure the car runs well are the crew members. They work on the mechanical problems, fix engines, replace tires and check the safety equipment. The person in charge of the crew is the crew chief.

Safety inspectors weigh and examine each car prior to the start of a race. The inspectors look for things that the pit crew may have forgotten.

And before a feature begins, the pace car leads the pack of cars around the track. When the pace car pulls off the track, the race has begun. This is signaled by the flagman. The flagman stands at the flag stand at the edge of the track. He is responsible for several things during a race. He uses different colored flags to tell the drivers what is happening. Some of the flag signals used are:

Green: Signals the beginning of a race.
Yellow: Signals the driver to slow down. Usually this means that there has been an accident on the track.
Red: Signals a bad accident.
Black: Signals a driver to bring his or her car

A day at the races!

into the pits. If the driver doesn't, he or she will be disqualified.

White: Signals the beginning of the last lap before the end of the race.

Checkered: Signals that the race is over.

Another important person is the announcer. The announcer sits in the control tower and informs the fans about what is happening on the track. The announcer knows the drivers, what cars they are racing, each one's current place in the race, and how well they have been performing during the season.

But perhaps the most important people at a race are the fans. They line up to buy the tickets. They come to cheer on their favorite racers. They pay the money that keeps the race track open.

Women on the Track

In the early days of racing, there weren't many women racing drivers. Women were accepted in rally racing and road racing but had a hard time getting started in stock car racing.

◀ A race official is always on hand to make sure that things go smoothly.

Alice "Racing Granny" Tatroe tears around the track at the New Smyrna Speedway.

For a long time, there weren't even rest rooms for women!

Although Janet Guthrie is the most famous woman driver, there were many before her. Drivers such as Louise Smith, Sara Christian and Ethel Flock Mobley left their marks as well. All three were able to break into Grand National racing. It was said that they knew how to broad-slide a car like a man and slam fenders with the best drivers around.

One colorful racer who drives at the New Smyrna Speedway and Orlando Speed World in Florida is Alice Tatroe. She is in her sixties and drives a late-model race car. Everyone at the tracks calls her Racing Granny. She is a popular driver with both kids and adults and is known internationally.

Stick with It

If you're a good young driver and people keep saying, "Just keep it up!" you've got a good chance at getting a sponsor. At first you may not get much money from a sponsor. You may get just enough to pay for tires. But that's a start.

Word gets around quickly in racing. When a promising new driver is on the scene people soon know it. A race car owner may read in the paper about how well you did at the track. He may hire you to drive for him. A company may hear about you and ask you to advertise its product.

If you're a good driver and willing to work hard, you'll make it into circle track racing. Then you're on your way to the big leagues and Winston Cup racing.

With hard work and patience a driver can find a sponsor and be on the way to winning big in circle track racing.

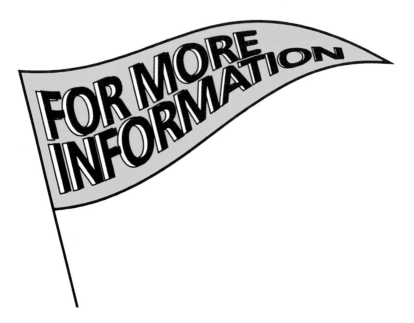

For more information on circle track racing, contact:

Dave Lecklitner
Mini-Stock Racing School
814 N. Main Street
Kissimmee, FL 32743

Duke Southard
Southard's School of High-Performance Driving
P.O. Box 1810
New Smyrna Beach, FL 32069

For information about speedways near you, look in the *National Speedway Directory*, which you can find at your local library. Or you can write to the following:

National Speedway Directory
666 Westway N.W.
Grand Rapids, MI 49504

FOR FURTHER READING

Chapin, Kim. *The Story of Stock Car Racing: Fast as White Lightning.* New York: Dial Press, 1981.

Crider, Curtis "Crawfish," as told to Don O'Reilly. *The Road to Daytona.* Ormand Beach, FL: Self-published, 1987.

Dolder, Bill. *Stock Car Racing.* New York: Gallery Books, 1990.

Engle, Lyle K. *The Complete Book of NASCAR Stock Car Racing.* New York: Four Winds Press, 1968.

Manning, Skip. *How to Go Grand National Racing.* Santa Ana, CA: Steve Smith Autosports, 1979.

Silber, Mark. *Racing Stock.* New York: Dolphin Books, 1976.

Wilkinson, Sylvia. *Dirt Tracks to Glory: The Early Days of Stock Car Racing as Told by the Participants.* New York: Algonquin Books, 1983.

horsepower 22—A means to describe units of power. One horsepower is equivalent to the use of 550 pounds of pressure per second.

hydraulic brakes 12—Brakes operated by the pressure of fluid in cylinders and connecting tubes.

ignition and coil 12—The ignition is the part of an internal combustion engine that ignites, or fires, the fuel in a cylinder. A coil conducts the flow of electricity to the spark plugs, which continually ignite the fuel to make the engine run.

jalopies 8, 14—Old or abandoned cars that were changed into race cars.

modifieds 10, 14, 21—Assembly-line cars that have been altered to make them competitive race cars.

pace car 6, 20, 32, 37—A car that sets an even speed for the beginning of a race.

pit crew 6, 25, 29, 36—The people who work on the race car to get it ready for a race.

purse 10—The amount of prize money a driver wins at a race.

qualifying rounds 5, 17—Competitions to determine which drivers will be allowed to race and in which starting positions. One car at a time does a single, timed lap around the track. The fastest car gets the best starting position, the next fastest gets second position, and so on.

roll bar 35—The steel bar in a race car that protects the driver in a turnover.

sponsor 25, 26, 36, 41—A person or business that pays expenses for a racing team in return for advertising.

stock car 13, 15, 16, 21, 22, 23, 39—A car used in circle track racing. Refers to the fact that the car has a standard, or stock, body, the same body it had when it came off the assembly line. Stock cars are modified for racing.